Evie the Mist Fairy

Thanks to real fairies
everywhere

Special thanks to
Sue Bentley

ISBN 0-439-81390-5

12 11 10 9 8 7 6 5 4   7 8 9 10 11/0

Printed in the U.S.A.   40

Evie the Mist Fairy

by Daisy Meadows
illustrated by Georgie Ripper

A
LITTLE APPLE
PAPERBACK

SCHOLASTIC INC.

New York Toronto London Auckland Sydney
Mexico City New Delhi Hong Kong Buenos Aires

The Fairyland Palace

Forest of

Candy Factory

The Village Hall

River

Wetherbury Village

Farm

Goblins green and goblins small,
I cast this spell to make you tall.
As high as the palace you shall grow.
My icy magic makes it so.

Then steal the rooster's magic feathers,
Used by the fairies to make all weathers.
Climate chaos I have planned
On Earth, and here, in Fairyland!

Contents

A Misty Morning   1

Magic in the Mist   15

Goblin in the Fog   27

Pogwurzel Plot   37

Goblin Pie   47

Back on Track   55

A Misty Morning

"Wake up, sleepyhead!" cried Kirsty
Tate, as she jumped out of bed and
started to get dressed.

Her friend, Rachel Walker, was asleep
in the extra bed in Kirsty's room. She
was staying with Kirsty and her parents
in Wetherbury. Sleepily, she rolled over
and opened her eyes. "I was dreaming

that we were back in Fairyland," she told
Kirsty. "The weather was mixed up —
sunny and snowing all at the same time —
and Doodle was trying to fix it." Doodle,
the magic weather rooster, had been on
Rachel's mind a lot lately, because she
and Kirsty were on an important mission
with the Weather Fairies!

Every day in Fairyland, the Weather Fairies used Doodle's magic tail feathers to make the weather. Each of the seven feathers controlled a different kind of weather, and each of the seven Weather Fairies was responsible for working with one specific feather. The system was perfect until mean Jack Frost sent his goblins to steal Doodle's magic feathers.

The goblins took the feathers into the human world, and when poor Doodle followed them out of Fairyland, he found himself transformed into a rusty weather vane. Since Rachel and Kirsty had found the Rainbow Fairies together, the Queen of the Fairies had asked them to help find and return Doodle's magic feathers, also.

In the meantime, Fairyland's weather was all mixed up — and the goblins had been using the feathers to cause trouble in the human world, too.

"Poor Doodle," Kirsty said, looking out the window at the weather vane on top of the old barn. Her dad had found Doodle lying in the park, and brought him home for their barn roof. "Hopefully we'll find another magic feather today," Kirsty continued. "We already have four of the stolen feathers. We just need to find the other three. Then Doodle will get his magic back!"

"Yes," Rachel agreed, brightening at

the thought. "But I have to go home in three days, so we don't have very long!" As she gazed out at the blue sky, a wisp of silvery mist caught her eye.

"Look — that cloud is shaped just like a feather!" she said.

Kirsty looked up, too. "I can't see anything."

Rachel looked again, but the wispy shape had disappeared. "Maybe I imagined it," she said, sighing.

The memory of the dream fizzed in her tummy like bubbles. It felt like a magical start to the day.

Rachel loved sharing fairy adventures

with Kirsty. The girls had met on vacation in Rainspell Island with their parents. That was when they had first helped the fairies. That time, Jack Frost had cast a nasty spell to send the Rainbow Fairies away from Fairyland, and the girls had helped all seven of them get home safely.

Now, Rachel and Kirsty hurried down to the kitchen. Mr. Tate was sitting at the table. He looked up and smiled at the girls. "Good morning! Did you sleep well?"

"Yes, thanks," Rachel replied. When she sat down, she saw a bright green flier on the kitchen table. It read: *Grand*

Fun Run, Green Wood Forest, Wetherbury.
Everyone welcome. She looked at the date.
"That's today."

"Yes. My mom's running in it," said
Kirsty.

"Most of the village will be racing.
Why don't you two go and watch?"

suggested Mr. Tate. "You could cheer
Mom on."

"OK," Rachel and Kirsty agreed
happily.

Maybe we could look for goblins on the way,

thought Rachel. She felt excited, and a little bit nervous. Goblins were mean creatures, and Jack Frost had cast a spell to make them bigger than normal. Luckily, the laws in Fairyland say that nothing can be taller than the King and Queen's fairy castle, so the goblins couldn't get too big. But they were still almost as tall as Rachel and Kirsty's shoulders.

Mr. Tate finished his cup of coffee and stood up. "I'm going to pick up Gran and take her to watch the race. We'll look for you there," he told the girls.

"OK, Dad. 'Bye!" Kirsty said with a wave.

Just then, Mrs. Tate hurried into the kitchen, wearing running shorts, a T-shirt, and sneakers. She smiled at Kirsty and

Rachel. "Sorry, I can't stop, girls. It's almost race time!"

"That's all right, Mom. We're right behind you," Kirsty said.

"We're coming to cheer you on," Rachel explained.

"See you at the woods, then!" Mrs. Tate called cheerfully as she headed out the door.

A few minutes later, Kirsty and Rachel left for Green Wood Forest, too.

"Let's take the path by the river," Kirsty suggested. "It's a little longer, but it's much prettier."

"Oh, yes! Maybe we'll see some ducklings," Rachel agreed.

As the girls walked up Twisty Lane, sunlight poured through the dancing tree branches. Spots of light speckled the road like golden coins. Soon Rachel and Kirsty reached the river. It was very pretty down by the water, where buttercups dotted the grass and cows grazed happily.

Rachel spotted little puffs of mist rising from the water. "Look! Do you think that could be fairy mist?" she asked.

"I'm not sure," Kirsty replied. "There's usually mist near water, isn't there?"

"Oh, yes, especially in the morning and at night," Rachel remembered. She felt a little disappointed, but brightened when she saw two swans gliding by. Dragonflies perched in the reeds beside the sparkling river. "It's a perfect day!" she said, smiling.

Kirsty nodded. Up ahead, she could see the edge of the forest. Something was shimmering on one of the tree branches. It looked like a silvery scarf, sparkling softly in the sunlight. "What's that?" she asked Rachel.

Rachel went over to look. "I don't know, but it's beautiful!" she replied. "It looks just like the tinsel that we use to decorate our Christmas tree."

"There's lots more of it on the other branches, too. Isn't it pretty?" Kirsty touched a strand of the strange, silvery stuff. It stuck to her fingers for a moment before melting away. "It feels cold!" Kirsty shivered, rubbing her hands together.

Rachel leaned forward for a closer look. Tiny silvery lights shimmered in the fine, silky threads. "This has to be fairy mist," she whispered excitedly.

Kirsty's eyes lit up. "I think you're right," she agreed. She looked toward a clump of tall oak trees. A wispy cloud of mist was floating gently down toward the trees from the sky. "More fairy mist!" Kirsty pointed out. "Come on!"

Magic in the Mist

The girls ran toward a path that led into the woods. They were out of breath by the time they stopped in the forest and looked around. Wispy mist clung to trees everywhere and coated the grass with tiny droplets. Every twig, leaf, and flower glowed with a soft silver light.

And where the sun reached down
through the trees, the fairy mist sparkled
with rainbow-colored light.

"Oh!" breathed Rachel. "It's so
beautiful!"

Kirsty stared in awe at the forest.
It looked almost as magical as
Fairyland!

Slowly, the girls moved forward. After

a few steps, Rachel realized that she
couldn't see very far ahead.

"This mist is getting thicker," she said.
"The goblin with the Mist Feather must
be hiding really close by."

Kirsty nodded as thick fog swirled
around them. "You're right, Rachel,"
she agreed. "I can hardly see a thing.
The goblin could be right behind us!"

Rachel rubbed her bare arms and shivered. Only a few minutes had passed, but as the mist grew thicker, the forest started to feel dark and unfriendly. Nothing glittered or gleamed anymore. The fog was settling around the girls like a cold blanket.

Shadowy figures moved up ahead. A man wearing a red T-shirt ran out in front of the girls, and another runner burst out of the trees. They were heading straight for each other. "Watch out!" cried Kirsty. But it was too late. *Crash!* The runners bumped right into each other.

"Sorry. Didn't see you there!" one of them said, rubbing his head.

"I've never seen fog like this in summer," replied the other one.

Rachel and Kirsty could hear rustles and bumps all around them. Voices echoed through the fog. Lots of runners were getting lost, and had to slow down and walk so they could avoid the trees.

"What a mess. This fog is ruining the race!" said Rachel.

The fog still seemed to be getting thicker. It hung over the trees, making them look dark and frightening.

Suddenly, something caught Kirsty's eye. "Over there!" she cried, pointing.

A bright light was moving toward them, shining like a lantern. Soon the girls could see that it was a tiny gleaming fairy.

"Oh!" gasped Kirsty. "It's Evie the Mist Fairy!"

"Hello again, Rachel and Kirsty," cried Evie in a bright, tinkly voice. She hovered in the air in front of them. The girls had met Evie in Fairyland, along with the rest of the Weather Fairies. She had long dark hair and violet eyes. She wore a fluttery lilac dress with purple boots, and her wand had a sparkly silver tip. Wisps of shimmering mist drifted from it.

"Oh, we're so happy to see you!" said Rachel.

"We really need your help," Kirsty added. "We're sure that the goblin with the Mist Feather is nearby."

"Yes!" agreed Evie, a frown on her tiny face. "And he's causing lots of misty mischief!"

"Could you leave a magic trail behind us as we go farther into the woods?" Rachel asked. "Then we can look for the goblin and still find our way back out."

Evie grinned. She waved her wand and a fountain of fairy dust shot out. It floated to the ground and formed a glittering path. "Of course! Now we won't get lost," she said.

"But we might bump into the runners," Kirsty pointed out. "Let's turn ourselves into fairies, Rachel. Then we can fly."

The Fairy Queen had given Rachel and Kirsty beautiful golden lockets full of fairy dust. The girls sprinkled themselves with the magic dust and shrank to fairy size. The trees seemed as big as giants' castles in the thick fog.

"I love being a fairy!" Kirsty sang out.

Rachel twisted around to look over her shoulder. There were her fairy wings on her back, shining delicately.

"Hooray!" Evie rose into the air, a trail of glittering mist streaming from her wand, and the two girls flew along behind her.

Below them, the runners were still stumbling through the fog. "Poor Mom. She was really looking forward to the race today. That goblin is spoiling everyone's fun," said Kirsty.

Suddenly, Rachel spotted a dark, hunched shape in the mist below. She waved to Kirsty and Evie. "Look down there," she called softly. "I think we found the goblin!"

Goblin in the Fog

They all floated down to investigate. The mist here was heavier and stickier. It pulled at Rachel's wings as she flew through it. "Oh, it's not a goblin — it's just a dead tree." She sighed, landing on the thick twisted trunk. She felt disappointed. The dark shape had looked just like a goblin from the air.

"We may not have found him yet," Kirsty whispered to her friend, "but I still think that the goblin isn't far away. The mist here smells musty, and it's harder to fly through."

Rachel fluttered her shiny wings. "Yes," she agreed. "It's like cold oatmeal."

Just then, they heard a gruff voice complaining nearby. "It's not fair! I'm cold and I'm lost and I'm hungry!" There was a loud sniff, like a pig snorting. "Poor me!"

Rachel, Kirsty, and Evie looked at one another in excitement.

"That's definitely a goblin!" declared Evie.

"Quick! Let's hide in that tree before he sees us," suggested Rachel.

They flew up and landed on the branch of a huge oak tree, then peered down through the thick green leaves. Sure enough, the goblin sat on a log below them. They could see the top of his head and his huge bony feet. They could

also hear a horrible gurgling sound, like slimy stuff going down a drain.

"Lost in this horrible forest! And I'm so hungry," moaned the goblin, clutching his rumbling tummy. "I'd love some toadstool stew and worm dumplings!"

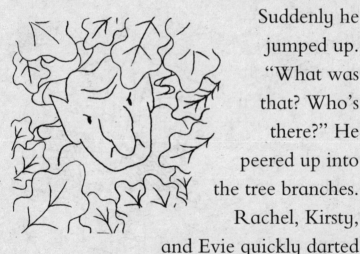

Suddenly he jumped up. "What was that? Who's there?" He peered up into the tree branches. Rachel, Kirsty, and Evie quickly darted behind the oak leaves. After a moment the goblin sat down on his log again. "Must have been a squirrel," he muttered. "Oh, I want to go home!"

The girls could see the goblin clearly now. He had bulging, crossed eyes and a big, lumpy nose like a potato. His arms were long and skinny but he had short legs and knobbly knees.

"Look what he's holding!" whispered Evie.

Kirsty and Rachel peered through the leaves and saw that the goblin clutched a

beautiful silvery feather with a lilac tip in his fingers. "The Mist Feather!" the girls exclaimed together.

Then Rachel frowned. "If the goblin's lost in the fog, why doesn't he use the magic feather to get rid of it?" she asked.

"Because he doesn't know how," Evie explained. "He's waving the feather all over the place without thinking — but he's only making more and more mist." It was true. The goblin was shaking the Mist Feather and mumbling to himself as thick swirls of fog drifted around him.

"Earwig fritters, beetle pancakes, lovely slug sandwiches . . ." he muttered wistfully.

Just then, one of the runners passed close by. The goblin shot to his feet and hid behind a tree. He was shaking so much that the three friends could hear his knees knocking together. "It's a . . . it's a Pogwurzel!" he whispered in panic.

As the sound of the runner's footsteps faded, the goblin peeked out again. "Phew! The Pogwurzel's gone." He flopped back down on the log, but kept looking around nervously.

Kirsty turned to Evie. "What is a Pogwurzel?" she asked.

Evie smiled, her violet eyes sparkling. "Pogwurzels are strange, magical, goblin-chasing monsters!" she replied.

Rachel looked at the fairy curiously. "Where do they live?" She and Kirsty had been to Fairyland a few times now. They had seen elves, goblins, and all kinds of fairies — but never a Pogwurzel.

Evie gave a peal of tinkly laughter. "Nowhere!" she said. "Because they don't exist! You see, goblin children can be really naughty. Their mothers tell

them that if they don't behave, a
Pogwurzel will come and chase them!"

Kirsty and Rachel laughed so hard that
they almost fell off the branch.

Then Rachel turned to Kirsty and Evie
in excitement. "I have an idea," she
whispered, her eyes shining. "I think I
know how we can get the Mist Feather
back!"

Pogwurzel Plot

Evie and Kirsty stared at Rachel. "Tell us!" they cried.

Rachel outlined her plan. "If we can convince the goblin that the forest is full of Pogwurzels, he'll do anything to escape. He'll want the mist cleared away so that he can find his way out of the woods. Since he's not clever enough to figure out how to use the Mist Feather himself, maybe we can convince him to give the feather to Evie and let her try."

Evie clapped her hands together in excitement. "Then I can keep it and take it back to Doodle!" she said. "It's a wonderful plan!"

"But I'm not sure how we can make the goblin think that there are hundreds of Pogwurzels in the forest," Rachel added.

The three friends sat quietly, thinking. Kirsty thought of her mom and the other runners trying to find their way along the race course. That gave her an idea. "I know how we can convince the goblin that there are Pogwurzels around!" she cried. "Evie, if you make us human-sized again, Rachel and I can creep up on the goblin from behind. Then we'll run past him, screaming that a Pogwurzel is chasing us!"

"Yes, that could work," Evie agreed.

"We'll have to be very convincing," Rachel added.

Evie nodded. "But you two can do it. I know you can," she said encouragingly.

The three friends flew silently down to the ground behind the oak tree. Evie waved her wand and the girls zoomed up to their normal height. "Ready?" asked Kirsty. "You bet," Rachel replied. The girls crept toward the goblin. They could see him sitting on his log, still muttering to himself. "Now!" whispered Rachel.

Kirsty dashed forward. "Help! Help! Save us from the Pogwurzel!" she shouted.

Rachel was right behind her. "It's huge and scary and won't leave us alone!" she cried.

The goblin leaped to his feet. His eyes

were as big as saucers. "What?" he gasped. "Who are you?"

Kirsty stopped. "Oh, my goodness, a goblin in Pogwurzel Wood!" she exclaimed, pretending to be surprised.

Rachel stopped, too. "You must be very brave," she declared.

The goblin's eyes flicked from Rachel to Kirsty. "Why?" he demanded shakily. "Are there many Pogwurzels around here?"

"Oh, yes," Kirsty chimed in. "Hundreds.

This forest is full of them. One of them was chasing us just now," she added, looking nervously over her shoulder. "He can't be far behind us."

Just then, Evie
fluttered down, her
wings shining in the
fog. "Pogwurzels
especially love to
catch goblins, you
know," she said.
The goblin's face
turned pale with fear.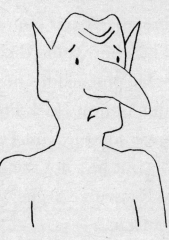

"If I were you, I'd get out of this forest
right now," Evie continued.

"But I can't," wailed the goblin. "The
fog is so thick that I can hardly see my
own toes!"

Evie smiled. "I'll help you," she said
sweetly. "Just give me that feather you're
holding. I'll use it to make a clear
pathway out of the forest for you."

Kirsty and Rachel could hardly

breathe. Their plan was working so far, but what would the goblin do next?

He pinched his nose thoughtfully. "I don't know. Jack Frost won't like it if I give you the Mist Feather."

"But he's not the one being chased by a Pogwurzel, is he?" Rachel pointed out quickly.

"The Pogwurzels in this forest are extra-big," Kirsty said. "And really, really mean."

"So is Jack Frost," the goblin said,

looking torn. "I think I'll keep the feather."

Kirsty's heart sank. It looked like the goblin was more stubborn than they had expected. She looked over at Rachel. Now what could they do?

Goblin Pie

Evie hovered close to the girls. "I have an idea," she whispered. "You distract the goblin, so he won't notice what I'm doing."

"What are you all talking about?" asked the goblin suspiciously.

"Oh, we just think we heard another Pogwurzel," Kirsty replied.

"Where?" the goblin spun around in fear. While his back was turned, Evie waved her wand in a complicated pattern. A big fountain of silver and violet sparks shot into a nearby bush, sending fairy magic there.

"I can hear it! It's coming this way!"
Rachel called out.

"I don't believe you," the goblin
sneered. "I can't hear it. You're just
trying to scare me. I bet you never
saw a Pogwurzel at all."

"Listen for yourself, then,"
Evie said.

The goblin turned his head
to one side and frowned in
concentration. Kirsty and
Rachel waited. They
weren't exactly sure what
Evie planned to do.

Suddenly a deep, scary
roar came from the
nearby bush. "*Raaghh!* I'm a
scary Pogwurzel! And I'm hungry for
Goblin Pie for my dinner!"

"Wow! Evie's magical voice is really scary," Kirsty whispered to Rachel.

The goblin stiffened. "Help me, Mommy!" he cried. "A Pogwurzel wants to eat me! I'm sorry I put those toenail clippings in your bed. I won't do it again. Help!" He stumbled behind Kirsty and Rachel, trying to hide. "Don't eat me, Mr.

Pogwurzel! Eat these girls instead. I bet they taste sweeter than I do!" Evie's magical voice came from the bush again. "I only eat goblins," it boomed. "Especially really naughty ones — like you!" The goblin squealed in alarm. His eyes bulged. He took the Mist Feather from his belt and thrust it at Evie. "Make the mist go away so I can get out of here," he begged. "I don't want to be made into Goblin Pie!"

Evie smiled, took the feather, and waved it expertly in the air. A clear path immediately appeared through the mist. The goblin gave one last terrified glance over his shoulder and then ran away as fast as he could, his big feet flapping noisily on the ground.

Kirsty, Rachel, and Evie laughed.

"Evie, that trick voice was fantastic!" Rachel said.

"It even scared *me*!"
Kirsty laughed.

"And now we have the
Mist Feather!" Evie
said, waving it
over her head.

Silver sparks shot
into the air and the mist
began to fade. Before long, the sun shone
down onto the forest again.

Rachel and Kirsty beamed. "We can
give Doodle another magic feather!"
Rachel said happily.

Evie flew up and did a joyful twirl in
the air. Silver and violet mist sparkled all
around her.

"And the race should be easier now,"
Kirsty added. "Let's see if we can spot Mom
before we head home to visit Doodle."

Back on Track

The three friends made their way toward the race course.

The forest paths were tinged with gold, and the smell of earth and leaves filled the air. Runners pounded along between trees marked with big red signs. Everyone could see where they were going now.

"You'd better hide on my shoulder," Rachel said to Evie.

Evie nodded and fluttered beneath Rachel's hair.

Suddenly, Kirsty spotted her mom dashing through the trees. Two other runners were close on her heels.

"Come on, Mom!" Kirsty shouted.

"You can do it!" yelled Rachel.

Kirsty's mom smiled and waved. "Not far to go now," she called.

Kirsty and Rachel jumped up and
down with delight. Evie
cheered, too, but only
Rachel could hear her
tiny voice.

"Looks
like your
mom's
doing
well," said
someone at
Kirsty's side.

"Dad! Gran! You're
here!" Kirsty exclaimed.

"And just in time. That fog held us up,"
said Mr. Tate. "Strange how it's
completely gone now. Almost like magic!"

Rachel and Kirsty looked at each other
and smiled.

"We're going to head home now,"
Kirsty told her dad.

"Sounds good," he replied. "Gran and
I will wait for Mom at the finish line."

On the way home, the girls enjoyed the
glorious sunshine, but Kirsty couldn't
help missing the sparkly fairy mist just a
little bit.

"Time to give Doodle his feather
back," said Rachel, as they reached
Kirsty's house. "I wonder if he'll say
something to us again." Every time the
girls had returned a tail feather,
Doodle had come briefly to
life and started to speak.
He'd given them part of a
message, and they couldn't
wait to hear the rest.
"I hope so," said Kirsty.

She repeated what Doodle had told them so far. "Beware! Jack Frost will come . . ."

Evie flew up to the barn roof. As she put the feather into place, the girls watched eagerly.

A fountain of copper and gold sparks
fizzed from Doodle's tail. The rusty old
weather vane disappeared and in its
place was a fiery magic rooster. Doodle
fluffed up his glorious feathers and turned
to stare at Rachel and Kirsty. "If his —"
he squawked. But before Doodle could
finish the message, his feathers turned to
iron and he became an ordinary weather
vane again.

Kirsty frowned. "Beware! Jack Frost
will come if his . . ." she said, repeating all
the words Doodle had said to them so far.

"Jack Frost will come if his *what*?"
Rachel wondered.

Kirsty shook her head. "We'll just have
to find the next feather and hope that
Doodle tells us," she said.

Evie nodded. "It's important to know
the whole message. Jack Frost is
dangerous," she warned.
"And now I must leave
you." She hugged
Rachel and Kirsty.
"Dear friends, thank you
for helping me."

"You're welcome,"
said Kirsty.

"Say hello to all our friends in Fairyland for us," added Rachel.

"I will," Evie promised, zooming up into the bright blue sky. Her wand left trails of silver mist in the air. Then she was gone.

Kirsty giggled. "I just remembered something the goblin said. I wonder whose toenail clippings he put in his mom's bed?" she said.

Rachel laughed happily. What an exciting day it had been. There were still two days of her visit left! Who knew what they would bring?

Crystal, Abigail, Pearl, Goldie, and Evie
have their magic feathers back. Now
Rachel and Kirsty must help

Storm the
Lightning
Fairy!

Magic in the Air

"I can't believe tomorrow is my last day here," groaned Rachel Walker. She was staying with her friend, Kirsty Tate, in Wetherbury for a week. The girls had gone on so many adventures together, they knew it was going to be hard to say good-bye.

Now, they were walking to the park,

excited to be outside. It had been pouring rain all night, but now the sun was shining again.

"Put your coats on, please," Mrs. Tate had told them before they left. "It looks awfully breezy out there!"

"It's been so much fun having you visit," Kirsty told her friend. "I don't think I'll ever forget this week, will you?"

Rachel shook her head. "No way," she agreed.

The two friends smiled at each other. It had been a very busy week. A snowy, windy, cloudy, sunny, misty week — thanks to Jack Frost and his goblins. The goblins had stolen the seven magic tail feathers from Doodle, Fairyland's weather rooster. The Weather Fairies used the feathers to control the weather, so now that the goblins had them, they were stirring up all kinds of trouble!

Rachel and Kirsty were helping the Weather Fairies get the feathers back. Without them, Doodle was just an ordinary weather vane! Kirsty's dad had found him lying in the park. He brought him home and put him on the roof of their old barn.

"Doodle has five of his magic feathers back now. I hope we find the last two before you have to go home," Kirsty said, pushing open the park gate.

Rachel nodded, but before she could say anything, raindrops started splashing down around them.

The girls looked up to see a huge

purple storm cloud covering the sun. The sky was getting darker by the second, and the rain was coming down harder and harder.

"Run, quick!" Kirsty shouted. "Before we get soaked!"

THINGS ARE GETTING Stormy!

A loose lightning bolt could cause terrible trouble in Wetherbury! Can Storm the Lightning Fairy and her magic feather get things under control—before it's too late?

SCHOLASTIC

www.scholastic.com

WF6

More Series You'll Fall in Love With

Heartland™
by Lauren Brooke

Nestled in the foothills of Virginia, there's a place where horses come when they're hurt. Amy, Ty, and everyone at Heartland work together to heal the horses—and form lasting bonds that will touch your heart.

www.scholastic.com/heartland

The AMAZING DAYS of ABBY HAYES®
by Anne Mazer

In a family of superstars, it's hard to stand out. But Abby is about to surprise her friends, her family, and most of all, herself!

www.scholastic.com/abbyhayes

DEAR DUMB DIARY
by Jim Benton

In Jamie Kelly's hilarious, candid (and sometimes not-so-nice) diaries, she promises everything she writes is true...or at least as true as it needs to be.

www.scholastic.com/deardumbdiary

Available Wherever Books Are Sold.

RAINBOW magic

Bring home all seven Rainbow Fairies

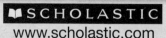

☐ 0-439-73861-X	Ruby the Red Fairy	$4.99
☐ 0-439-74465-2	Amber the Orange Fairy	$4.99
☐ 0-439-74466-0	Sunny the Yellow Fairy	$4.99
☐ 0-439-74467-9	Fern the Green Fairy	$4.99
☐ 0-439-74684-1	Sky the Blue Fairy	$4.99
☐ 0-439-74685-X	Inky the Indigo Fairy	$4.99
☐ 0-439-74686-8	Heather the Violet Fairy	$4.99

Available wherever you buy books, or use this order form.

Scholastic Inc., P.O. Box 7502, Jefferson City, MO 65102

Please send me the books I have checked above. I am enclosing $_____ (please add $2.00 to cover shipping and handling). Send check or money order — no cash or C.O.D.s please.

Name_____ Birth date_____

Address_____

City_____ State/Zip_____

Please allow four to six weeks for delivery. Offer good in U.S.A. only. Sorry, mail orders are not available to residents of Canada. Prices subject to change.

■SCHOLASTIC
www.scholastic.com